Uncle Boris and Maude

Doubleday & Company, Inc., Garden City, New York

Uncle Boris and Maude

By Marjorie Weinman Sharmat

Pictures by Sammis McLean

For Natalie and Stanley Becker

in deepest friendship

Library of Congress Catalog Number 78-18565

ISBN 0-385-12946-7 Trade
ISBN 0-385-12947-5 Prebound
Text copyright © 1979 by Marjorie Weinman Sharmat
Illustrations copyright © 1979 by Sammis McLean

Maude Mole woke up early.

"I have one hundred and eleven things

to do today," she said.

"Lucky me!"

Maude baked crunchy worm cookies,

dug a new room,

played the piano,

6   wrote in her diary

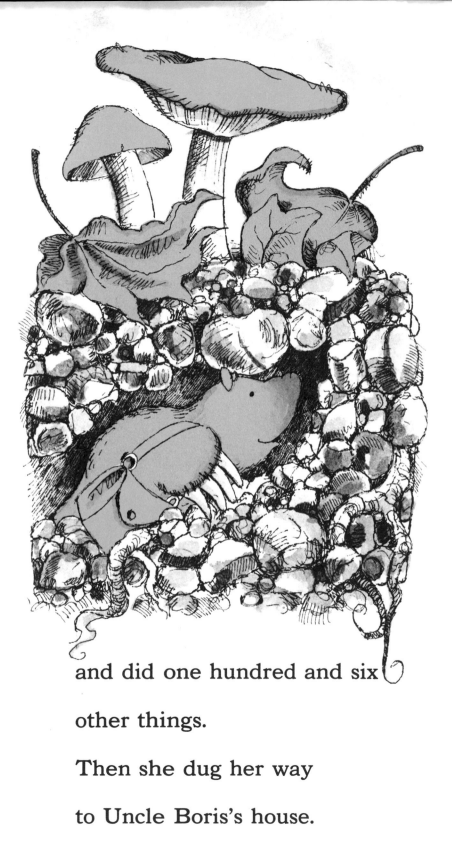

and did one hundred and six

other things.

Then she dug her way

to Uncle Boris's house.

7

"How are you?" asked Uncle Boris.

"Great," said Maude.

"I did one hundred and ten things

today. And then I came over here.

That's one hundred and eleven."

Maude kissed Uncle Boris.

"How are you, Uncle Boris?"

"How am I? I am bored,"

said Uncle Boris.

9

did not think

you were ever bored,"

said Maude.

"Well, once in a while I am,"

said Uncle Boris.

"It seems to happen

on Tuesdays and Fridays."

"Today is Friday," said Maude.

"Yes, and today I am bored,"

said Uncle Boris.

"Well, cheer up," said Maude.

"Tomorrow is Saturday.

Tomorrow your boredom

will be all finished."

Maude clapped her hands.

"Isn't it exciting to think

that tomorrow you won't be bored

anymore?" she said.

"Until next Tuesday," said Uncle Boris.

"Then I will have another

whole day of it."

"Maybe your mind does not

have enough to do,"

said Maude.

"Oh, my mind is very busy,"

said Uncle Boris. "Whatever you

can think about, my mind has

already thought about it.

That's how busy my mind is."

"Maybe your body should

be busy," said Maude.

"Oh it is," said Uncle Boris.

"Every day I walk five miles

before breakfast. And I skip

and jump and do yoga

and stand on my head.

That's busy, Maude."

"Yes, that's a busy body,"

said Maude.

"Do you mind if I yawn?"

asked Uncle Boris.

"What a great idea!" said Maude.

"You can yawn

in exciting new ways.

Close your eyes, open your eyes,

jump up and down,

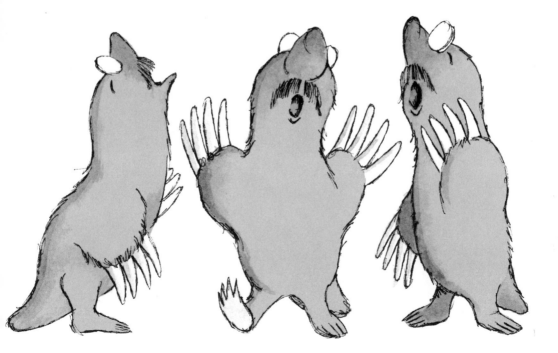

don't jump up and down,

yawn fast, yawn slowly."

Uncle Boris yawned

all the ways he could think of.

He yawned twenty different ways.

He even did a somersault

while he yawned.

When he was finished,

he yawned and said,

"That was boring."

Maude sighed.

"Everything will be all right

on Saturday," she said.

She kissed Uncle Boris

and went home.

On Saturday Maude's telephone rang.

She answered it.

"This is Uncle Boris,"

said Uncle Boris.

"I'm in trouble.

It's happening on Saturday now.

I am bored on Saturday."

"I will help you," said Maude.

"I will be right over."

Maude thought,

"I will give Uncle Boris a surprise.

A surprise can never be boring

because it is surprising.

I will give Uncle Boris

the cookies I baked for myself."

Maude put the cookies in a box.

She wrapped the box with paper

that had pictures of flowers and trees

and worms all over it.

Then she tied the present

with a big bow

and took it to Uncle Boris's house.

"Uncle Boris, Uncle Boris!" she called.

"I have a surprise for you."

"Oh, I am all excited,"

said Uncle Boris.

"Today isn't my birthday.

And it isn't Christmas.

Today is just today.

Why did you give me a surprise

on a day that is just a day?"

"A surprise will make it

a special day," said Maude.

"Why don't you

open your present?"

"Maybe tomorrow," said Uncle Boris,

"if the weather is good."

"What does the weather

have to do with it?"

asked Maude.

"Nothing," said Uncle Boris.

"But when I open my present

the surprise will be gone

and I will be bored again.

So would you please take

the present home with you?"

"Well, all right," said Maude.

"I will take it home
right now."
Maude took the present
and dug her way home.

She made supper, listened to the radio,

washed her fur and went to bed.

At six o'clock in the morning

her telephone rang.

She answered it.

"This is Uncle Boris,"

said Uncle Boris.

"I want to open my present."

"Now?" said Maude. "At six o'clock

in the morning?"

"Yes," said Uncle Boris.

"I can't sleep because

I don't know what it is.

May I come to your house

and open it?"

"If you really want to,"

said Maude.

"Oh, it's a box of cookies!

Thank you very much."

Uncle Boris dug his way

to Maude's house.

"Good-bye surprise, hello boredom,"

he said. And he opened the present.

Uncle Boris sat down.

"I like cookies. I love cookies.

But the surprise is over.

I am back to bored."

"No!" said Maude.

"I have another idea."

Maude pointed up.

"There is a snowstorm up there.

And we are going out into it."

"Wonderful!" said Uncle Boris.

"I have never been in a snowstorm."

Uncle Boris and Maude dug their way up.

"Snow!" said Uncle Boris.

"A blizzard!"

"Where are you?" yelled Maude.

"I can't see you."

"Over here!" said Uncle Boris.

And he yawned.

"Isn't this exciting!" said Maude.

"Snow on my nose. Wind in my face.

Everything tingles.

This is the best blizzard ever!"

"No," said Uncle Boris.

"This is a cold, sloppy,

wet, boring blizzard.

Let's go back inside."

Uncle Boris and Maude

dug their way down

to Maude's house.

"I'm sorry," said Uncle Boris,

and he fell asleep.

Maude picked up the telephone book

and opened it to the Yellow Pages.

She looked at the ads under M.

"Monsters, monsters.

Ah, here's one.

Fourteen feet, eight inches tall.

Nine hundred and eighty pounds

before breakfast.

Eleven hundred and sixty pounds

after breakfast.

Can shriek, scream and grunt."

Maude dialed the monster's number.

"GR-O-O-OWL!"

said a voice.

"Oh, hello," said Maude.

"I need a monster.

My Uncle Boris is bored.

I think if he met you

he would not be bored anymore."

"GR-O-O-OWL! GR-O-O-OWL!"

said the voice.

"I'm sure he would not

be bored anymore," said Maude.

"We're at 8 Mole Street.

Please come right over."

"GR-O-O-OWL!"

"I guess he said yes," said Maude.

A few minutes later

Maude heard a loud sound.

THUMP! THUMP!

Uncle Boris woke up.

"Somebody strong is

at your door," he said.

CRASH!

"Somebody strong is

standing on your door,"

said Uncle Boris.

"GR-O-O-OWL."

The monster jumped up and down.

He grabbed Uncle Boris's cookies

and ate them up

in one gulp.

"Oh!" said Maude.

"Please pick up the door,

whoever you are," said Uncle Boris.

"Doesn't he scare you, Uncle Boris?"

asked Maude.

"Ho-hum," said Uncle Boris

as he walked around the monster.

"My, you're a big one."

"GR-O-O-OWL."

"Nice voice, too," said Uncle Boris.

"But you're fat.

And you've got rotten teeth.

Give up the cookies

and the midnight snacks.

I'll get you some skim milk."

"GR-O-O-OWL."

"You're welcome," said Uncle Boris,

and he walked into the kitchen.

The monster turned to Maude

and shrugged.

"I give up," he said.

And he left.

"What a boring guest,"

said Uncle Boris

as he came back into the room.

"All he could say was 'growl.'"

Maude sat down on the floor.

"I give up, too," she said.

"What do you mean?"

asked Uncle Boris.

"I am bored

with your being bored,"

said Maude. "I am going

to sit and do nothing."

"But you did

one hundred and eleven things

just the other day,"

said Uncle Boris.

"That was before

I was bored," said Maude.

"But you must do *something*,"

said Uncle Boris.

"I don't feel like it,"

said Maude.

"Oh, dear,"

thought Uncle Boris.

Uncle Boris was thinking,

"This is all my fault.

Maude tried so hard

to help me

that now she needs me

to help her."

Uncle Boris picked up the door

that the monster knocked down.

"Let's put your door

back in place," he said.

"Well, maybe we could do that

together," said Maude.

She and Uncle Boris

put the door

back in place.

Then Uncle Boris said,

"That monster tracked snow

into your house.

You should clean your rug."

"Well, all right," said Maude.

Maude started to scrub her rug.

"There is enough dirt here

for two to clean,"

said Uncle Boris.

"I will help."

Uncle Boris sang a tune

while he scrubbed.

"Scrubbing makes my claws

feel good," he said.

"Scrub, scrub, rub.

Rub, rub, scrub,"

he sang.

When he finished scrubbing,

Uncle Boris said,

"The monster ripped your curtains."

Uncle Boris and Maude

sewed the curtains.

Then Uncle Boris said,

"Your whole house needs work.

And all the tunnels

leading to it."

"Uncle Boris, you are right,"

said Maude.

Uncle Boris and Maude worked

for a week

and rested and dreamed

and painted pictures

and told mole jokes

and played the piano

and baked

crunchy worm cookies.

Suddenly Uncle Boris shouted,

"I forgot something!"

"What?" asked Maude.

"I forgot to be bored,"

said Uncle Boris.

"I forgot through Tuesday,

Friday and Saturday.

Maybe I will

never be bored again!"

Maude hugged Uncle Boris.

Then he went home.

The next day Maude did

one hundred and twelve things

and Uncle Boris did

two hundred and twenty-nine.

The next day Maude did

one hundred and twelve things

and Uncle Boris did

two hundred and twenty-nine.

MARJORIE WEINMAN SHARMAT is the author of many beloved books for children. She grew up in Portland, Maine, and now lives in Tucson, Arizona, with her husband and children.

SAMMIS McLEAN grew up in Cohasset, Massachusetts, and graduated from the Art Institute of Boston. He now lives in New York City, and has illustrated two other picture books for children, *I Been There* and *Super-Vroomer!*